WARNING!

Scaredy Squirrel insists that everyone put on No.65 sunscreen before reading this book.

For Sergio, Nelson and Pablo, who bravely
helped us build our very own beach getaway

Published by
Happy Cat Books
An imprint of Catnip Publishing Ltd
14 Greville Street
London
EC1N 8SB

First published in paperback in 2009
1 3 5 7 9 10 8 6 4 2

First published in Canada by Kids Can Press Ltd, 29 Birch Avenue.
Toronto, ON M4V 1E2

Text and illustrations copyright © Melanie Watt, 2008

The moral rights of the author/illustrator have been asserted

A CIP catalogue for this book is available from the British Library

ISBN 978-1-905117-87-1

The artwork for this book was rendered digitally in Photoshop
The text is set in Potato Cut

Printed in China

www.catnippublishing.co.uk

Scaredy Squirrel

at the beach

by Melanie Watt

TAKE A BEACH HOLIDAY!

Scaredy Squirrel never goes to the beach. He'd rather holiday at home alone where it's safe than risk being surrounded by the wrong crowd.

A few crowds Scaredy Squirrel wouldn't want to be caught in the middle of:

flocks of seagulls

tribes of jellyfish

herds of sea monsters

packs of pirates

tons of falling coconuts

mobs of lobsters

So he's perfectly
happy to build his very
own private beach.

Scaredy Squirrel's Guide to Building a Safe Beach

What you need to get started:

paper and crayons

1 stick

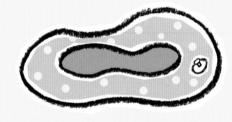

1 inflatable pool

1 torch

1 bag of kitty litter

1 plastic flamingo

1. Draw beach "scenery."

2. Use stick to hold upright.

3. Cover ground with "sand."

4. Inflate "ocean."

5. Turn on "sunlight."

6. Install beach "wildlife"...

And ENJOY!

TOCK TOCK TOCK

NO GERMS!

It looks like a beach and feels like a beach, but it doesn't sound like one. Scaredy Squirrel notices something's missing: the soothing sound of the ocean!

THE SOLUTION:
Make a quick trip to the REAL beach and find a seashell that fits the description below.

SEASHELL
(Quality and Performance Chart)

☑ germ-free

☑ shiny exterior

☑ crystal clear ocean sound

RED ALERT! Seashell must NOT, I repeat, NOT be occupied!

But travelling to the **REAL** beach requires careful planning.

First, get a passport.

NO GERMS!

-PASSPORT-

Family: rodent
Type: flying squirrel
First name: Scaredy
Middle name: Orville
Last name: Squirrel
Initials: S.O.S.
Place of birth: nut tree

SUBJECT HAS NEVER TRAVELLED

S///OOO//SOS//UNKNOWN)))

Second, draw a map ...

BEACH MAP

(MISSION: Operation Seashell)

7:00 a.m.: Enter box and wait
(don't forget passport)

7:30 a.m.: Get picked up by mail van
(verify passport)

8:42 a.m.: Arrive at beach and wait until
the coast is clear
(don't lose passport)

11:42 a.m.: Exit box and find seashell
(hold passport)

1:49 p.m.: Enter box and wait for pick-up
(check passport)

6:00 p.m.: Get delivered back to nut tree
(put away passport)

Caution: falling coconuts have a mind of their own — they can knock you out without warning.

Important: sea monsters are camera shy, so keep camera close by.

Seashell should be here.

AHOY MATEY! Watch fer pirates. AARRR! They'll make ye walk the plank!

Stay away from tribes of jellyfish: you'll be stung by how sneaky they can be.

Never trust a mob of lobsters: they are a pinch territorial and are eager to snap.

Careful: birds of a feather flock together. Seagulls can drop by at any time!

N
W   E
S

And last but not least, travel light and dress accordingly.

SCAREDY'S BEACHWEAR

This squirrel is a trained professional. Don't try this at home!

Exhibit A:
Protective headgear for falling coconuts

Exhibit B:
Protective eye patch to fool pirates

Exhibit C:
Protective floatation device to prevent sinking

Exhibit D:
Protective camera to discourage sea monsters

Exhibit E:
Protective compass to avoid getting lost

Exhibit I:
Protective french fry to distract seagulls

Exhibit H:
Protective oven mitts to block germs

Exhibit G:
Protective rubber band to tame lobsters

Exhibit F:
Protective footgear to shield from jellyfish

Remember, if all else fails, play dead and send an SOS!

The next morning, as planned, Scaredy Squirrel jumps into the box.

At 7:30 a.m. he gets picked up. They drive ...

... and drive.

WELCOME TO THE BEACH!

At 8:42 a.m. Scaredy gets dropped off and waits ... and waits.

Scaredy Squirrel panics and . . .

Finally Scaredy Squirrel realizes that the perfect seashell is right under his nose.

Surrounded by friendly people, he decides to join the crowd.

SURF'S UP!

Scaredy Squirrel builds sand castles ...

takes pictures ...

SHALLOW WATER

floats around
in the ocean ...

and sunbathes
with the others.

He forgets all about the flocks of
seagulls, tribes of jellyfish, herds of
sea monsters, packs of pirates, tons of
falling coconuts and mobs of lobsters.

He's glad to be part of the crowd!

Back home, after a day of fun in the sun, Scaredy Squirrel's inspired to make one more important addition to his own beach . . .

A CROWD!

garden
gnomes

P.S. As for Scaredy's next visit to the beach, it might be sooner than he thinks ...

RED ALERT!